Welcome to JURASSIC PARK ™

Adapted by Mike Teitelbaum
From a Screenplay by Michael Crichton and David Koepp
Based on the Novel by Michael Crichton

A GOLDEN BOOK • NEW YORK
Western Publishing Company, Inc., Racine, Wisconsin 53404

JURASSIC PARK™ & © 1993 Universal City Studios, Inc., and Amblin Entertainment, Inc. All rights reserved. Licensed by MCA/Universal Merchandising, Inc. Printed in the U.S.A. No part of this book may be reproduced or copied in any form without written permission from the copyright owner. All other trademarks are the property of Western Publishing Company, Inc. Library of Congress Catalog Card Number: 93-77752 ISBN: 0-307-12796-6/ISBN: 0-307-62796-9 (lib. bdg.)   A MCMXCIII

Jurassic Park is a huge natural park located on a mysterious fog-covered island. In this very special place, scientists have found a way to bring dinosaurs back to life!

Tourists ride through the park's beautiful mountains and lush jungles in electrically powered, remote-controlled cars. Visitors are practically face-to-face with living dinosaurs! The most dangerous animals are separated from the people by high-voltage electric fences.

Today several people are coming to Jurassic Park for a special private tour before the park officially opens. They include Dr. Alan Grant and Dr. Ellie Sattler, both paleontologists—scientists who learn about life in the past by digging up and studying fossils. Many fossils are dinosaur bones.

On the way to join the others at the park's Visitor Center, the scientists catch a glimpse of a living dinosaur—a brachiosaur. This huge plant-eater, or herbivore, stands 35 feet high, with a 20-foot neck and a very long tail. The friendly brachiosaur spends most of its time eating leaves and branches from tall trees.

When Dr. Grant and Dr. Sattler arrive at the center,
John Hammond, the man who is in charge of the park,
shows them the room where dinosaur eggs are hatched.
They are just in time to see one of the eggs hatch, and
they get their first look at a living baby dinosaur.

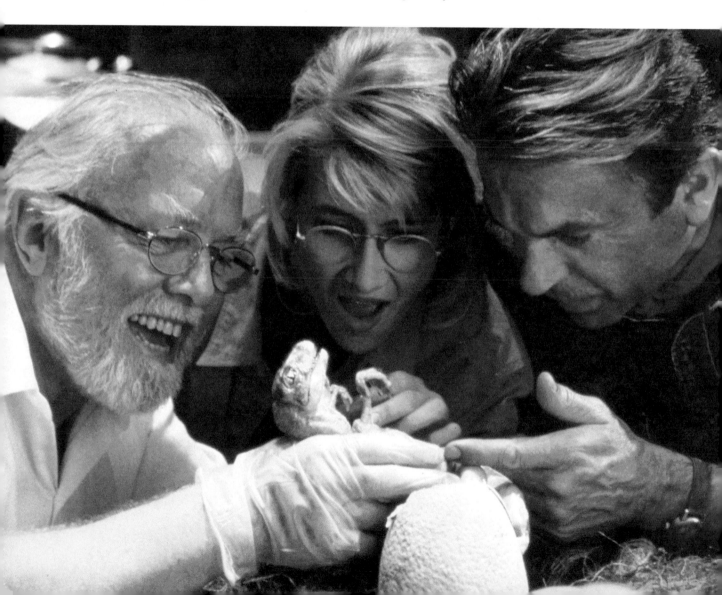

Joining Dr. Grant and Dr. Sattler are Lex and Tim,
John Hammond's grandchildren. Twelve-year-old Lex is a
computer whiz. She is amazed by the huge computer
system that controls and monitors Jurassic Park.

Her nine-year-old brother, Tim, is a dinosaur
enthusiast. He can hardly wait to talk with Dr. Grant
about the incredible world of dinosaurs.

When the tour begins, Dr. Grant, Dr. Sattler, Tim, and
Lex set out in two electric cars.

Their first stop is the *Dilophosaurus* exhibit.

The dilophosaur is about 4 feet tall and built like a kangaroo. It has a brilliantly colored crest that fans out around its neck when it becomes alarmed.

The dilophosaur attacks by spitting venom that can blind and paralyze a victim from as far away as 20 feet.

Next the group comes to the *Triceratops* exhibit. About the size of an elephant, this slow-moving dinosaur has a big head with three horns. It eats grass and plants.

When the visitors spot an animal lying on the ground, they get out of the cars to take a closer look.

It is a *Triceratops* dinosaur that seems to be sick. After examining it, Dr. Sattler volunteers to stay behind to help a park attendant care for the unfortunate creature.

Dr. Grant and the children continue the tour.

The electric cars move on to the *Tyrannosaurus rex* exhibit. *Tyrannosaurus rex* is the most ferocious of all dinosaurs. This meat-eater, or carnivore, stands 25 feet tall and 40 feet long. With its huge powerful jaws, it can swallow a large animal whole!

Suddenly the power in Jurassic Park goes out!
The electric cars stop running, and the electric fence that holds the *Tyrannosaurus rex* becomes useless. The mighty *T. rex* gets loose!

Dr. Grant and the children are trapped in their car
when the *T. rex* spots them!

As the huge beast attacks, Tim, Lex, and Dr. Grant
manage to scramble out of the car and down the side of
a mountain to safety. And not a minute too soon—the
car is destroyed in an instant.

Exhausted, the three visitors stop to rest after their frightening encounter with the *T. rex*.

During this time, Tim has a chance to talk about dinosaurs with Dr. Grant.

Though the children are still tired, Dr. Grant knows that they must move on.

With their car wrecked and the power in Jurassic Park still out, they must now walk many miles back to the park's Visitor Center.

When it starts to get dark, the three travelers find
shelter for the night high up in a huge tree. This keeps
them safe from any meat-eating dinosaurs that might
wander by.

Suddenly they hear a sound. Something is moving
through the jungle, coming right toward them!

Fortunately, it's only a brachiosaur.

Everyone is delighted to be so close to a real dinosaur. They feed leaves from the tree to the gentle giant.

The next morning the weary three make their way back to the Visitor Center, only to discover that dangerous raptors have gotten loose and are roaming the area.

Raptors, or *Velociraptors*, are deadly carnivores. They stand about 6 feet tall, can run at speeds up to 60 miles per hour, and they have a razor-sharp claw on each foot. They are the most cunning dinosaurs in all of Jurassic Park.

Dr. Grant has to think fast. He hurries Tim and Lex into the Visitor Center's large kitchen, where he thinks they will be safe. Then he goes to find Dr. Sattler.

But the children are not really safe. Several raptors are lurking in the kitchen!

When Tim and Lex realize that the raptors are ready to attack, they try to stay out of sight. But the clever raptors soon discover their hiding place.

The dangerous creatures chase the children around the kitchen.

Tim and Lex finally outsmart the raptors by luring them into the freezer. Lex slams the door shut, trapping the dinosaurs inside.

The children rush to the lobby, where they are reunited with their grandfather and the scientists.

Finally, after much danger and excitement, the visitors and John Hammond are helicoptered off the island. As they head for home, everyone realizes that Hammond's dream to open Jurassic Park never will—or should—come true.